One Small Fish

JOANNE RYDER

illustrated by

CAROL SCHWARTZ

Morrow Junior Books
New York

The text for *One Small Fish* is an expanded adaptation of a poem called
"Inside the Science Lab," copyright © 1981 by Joanne Ryder.
"Inside the Science Lab" first appeared in *Breakfast, Books, and Dreams*,
an anthology published by Frederick Warne and Co., Inc., in 1981.

Gouache and airbrush were used for the full-color artwork.
The text type is 16-point Chelmsford.

Printed in Hong Kong by South China Printing Company (1988) Ltd.
1 2 3 4 5 6 7 8 9 10

Library of Congress Cataloging-in-Publication Data
Ryder, Joanne.
One small fish / Joanne Ryder ; illustrated by Carol Schwartz.
p. cm.
Summary: While sitting in science class on a Friday afternoon, a
student watches all kinds of sea creatures move about the room.
ISBN 0-688-07059-0.—ISBN 0-688-07060-4 (lib. bdg.)
[1. Marine animals—Fiction. 2. Schools—Fiction.] I. Schwartz,
Carol, ill. II. Title.
PZ7.R959On 1993
[E]—dc20 92-21563 CIP AC

To the dearest of sea dreamers,
Franny Yep and Simon Labov,
and to all of you who daydream too
                                    J. R.

For Lynn—teach with imagination
                                    C. S.

On Friday afternoon
we file into
the science room
like rows of ants
and find our seats
among the plants,
among the tanks
of lizards, insects,
snakes and fish.

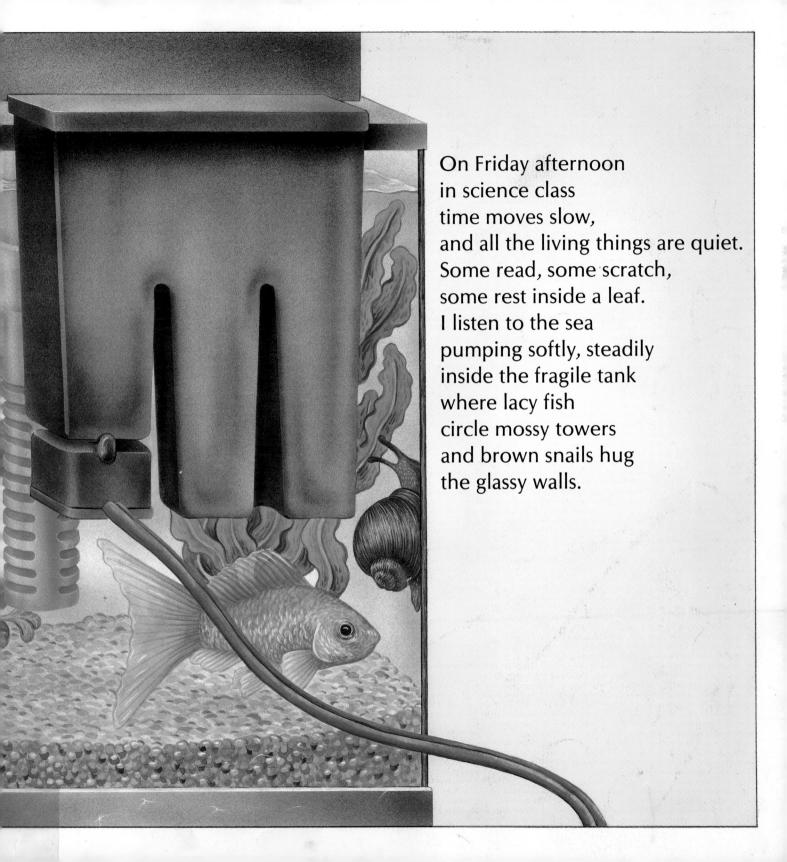

On Friday afternoon
in science class
time moves slow,
and all the living things are quiet.
Some read, some scratch,
some rest inside a leaf.
I listen to the sea
pumping softly, steadily
inside the fragile tank
where lacy fish
circle mossy towers
and brown snails hug
the glassy walls.

I listen to the sea
that beats and beats
quietly inside me—
and dream of waves,
of water swirling
higher and higher
until our room
is sunken
like a ship
in a shining sea.

While everybody studies,
I watch pale octopi
skitter from the pages
to the smooth dark floor,
where shimmery fish
nibble sweetly
at a piece of fallen chalk.

No one notices the eels
swimming single file
down the rows
to deeper waters...
or sees that right behind
our teacher's head
shy sea horses bob
up
        and down
                        and up
peeking at me.

Dark shadows glide above me as seals touch flippers to tails playing tag.

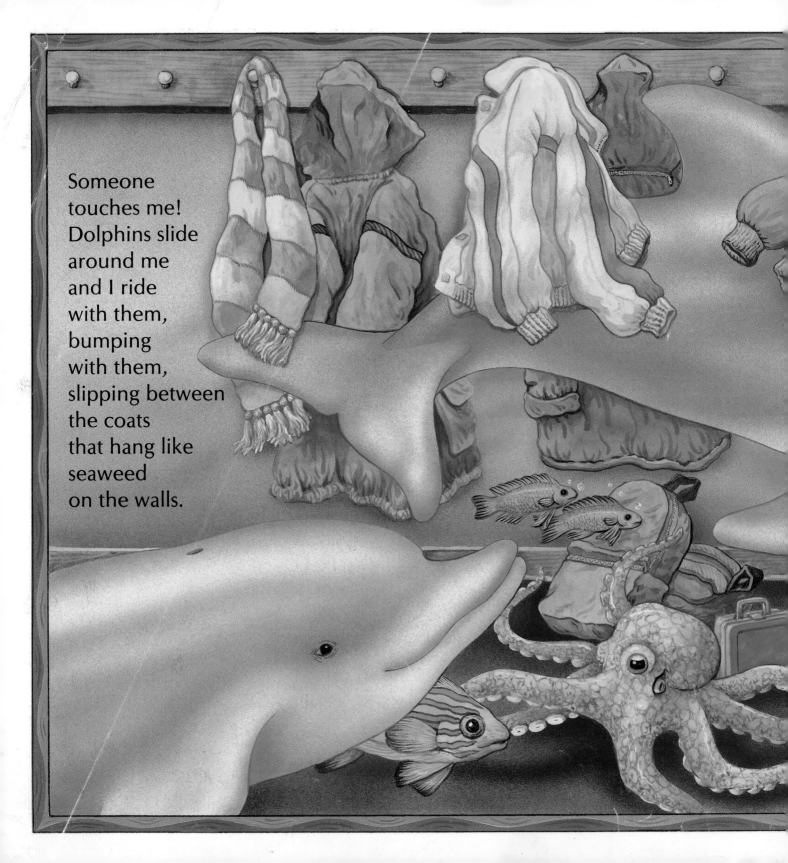

Someone
touches me!
Dolphins slide
around me
and I ride
with them,
bumping
with them,
slipping between
the coats
that hang like
seaweed
on the walls.

A school of fish,
playful and quick,
dashes through
the open door,
darting this way
and that way,
racing toward me,
shooting at me—
then turning.

Only one small fish
slows, draws closer.
I hold my breath
and feel pale fins,
eyelash soft,
brushing my skin.
One small fish
tickles me,
flickers around
my face,
teasing me
to watch it,
to catch it
with my eyes.
It plays with me
until I blink
and it is gone.

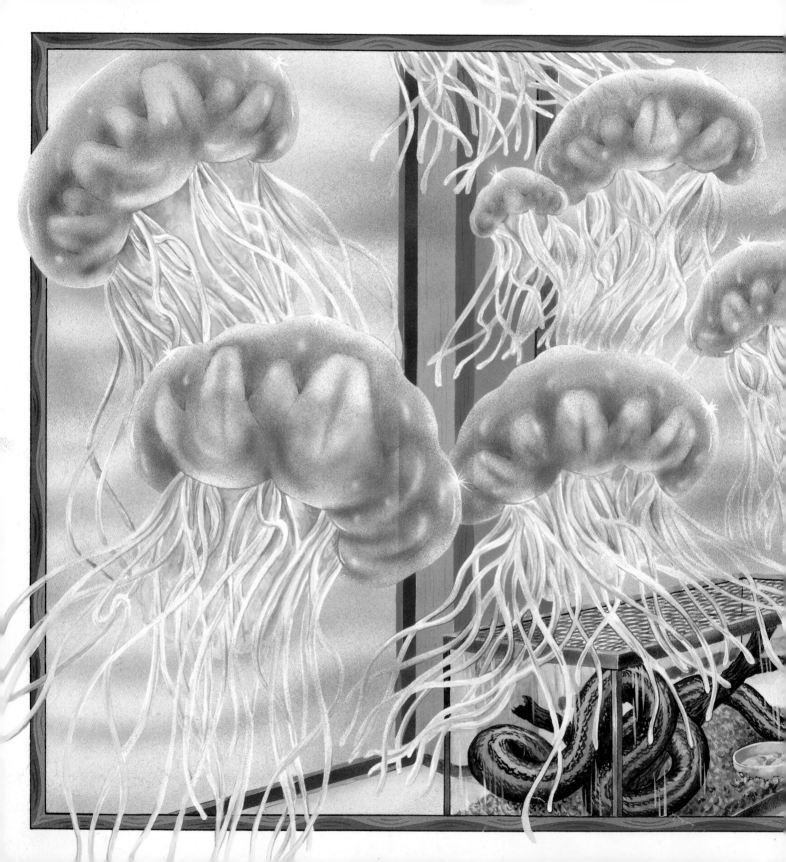

I look around
but all the sea
is still and quiet.
Near the windows
jellyfish ripple,
gently drifting
clear as glass,
their streamers
sparkling
in the sunlight.

Ever so slowly,
bright starfish
climb the walls
and curl
around the globe.
Ever so silently,
blue crabs creep,
arms stretched wide,
in and out
of open bookbags,
chewing test papers
in their tiny mouths.

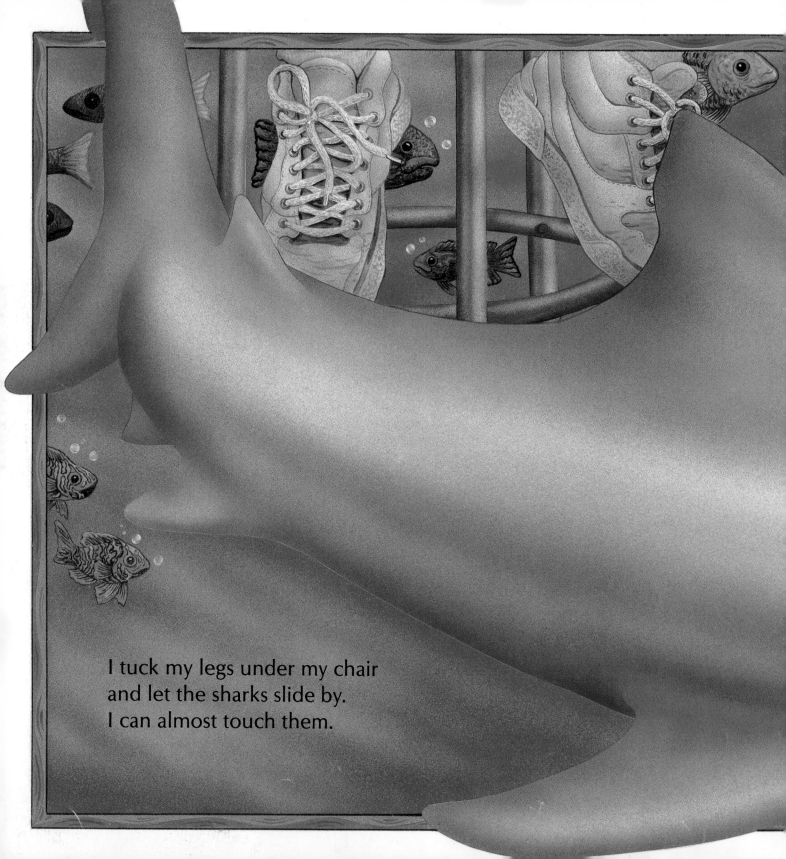

I tuck my legs under my chair
and let the sharks slide by.
I can almost touch them.

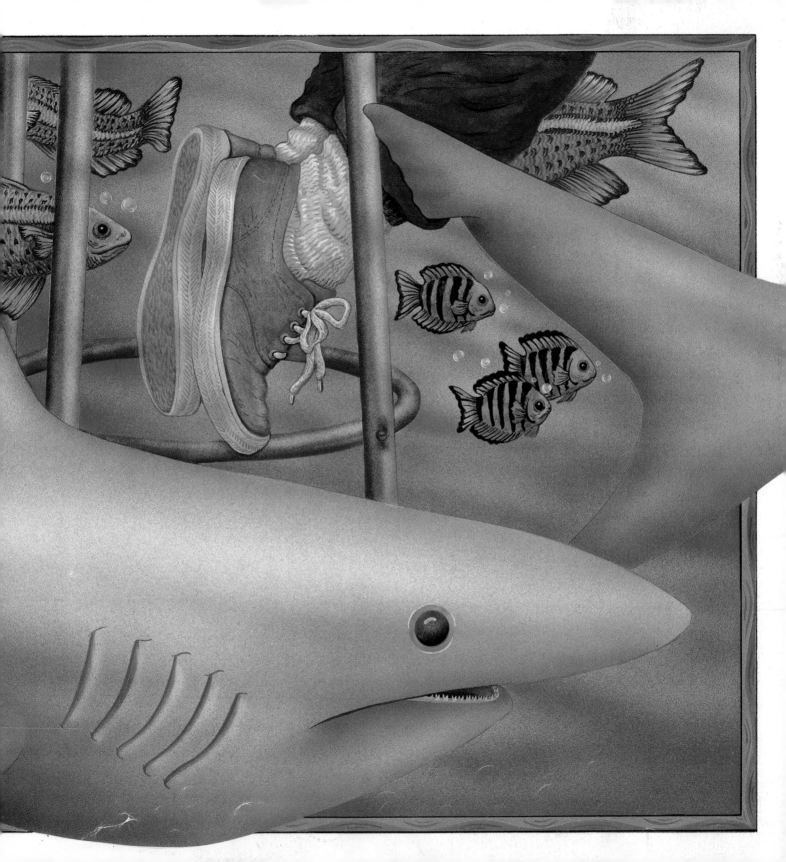

BRINNNNNNNG!!
The cold, sharp bell
breaks Friday's spell,
chasing me into the hall
and all the sea things
into hidden corners.

I leave the sea behind,
waiting till next week,
but in the distance
I know…

one small fish
follows me home.